Cat Mandoo
The Feline Who Flew

by Alexis Kasden

illustrations by Lynda Kodwyck

PAGE PUBLISHING, INC.
Conneaut Lake, PA

First originally published by Page Publishing 2019

ISBN 978-1-68456-340-1 (pbk)
ISBN 978-1-68456-341-8 (digital)

Printed in the United States of America

Dedicated to all the animals who have been
good enough to spend their lives with us:
Jack and Siam
Harry
Spice and Starboy
Dewy
Harley and Kit Carson
The O Es, Chloe and Zoe
And our thirteen-year-old goldfish, FishWish

CHAPTER 1

The Happy Cat with the Big Dream

Cat Mandoo was a very happy Tuxedo feline who lived in a very happy home. Mr. and Mrs. Joyful—his human parents who loved him dearly, four fish, and forty-four flowering plants lived there too. Sunshine—even, it seemed, on the cloudiest days—filled this happy place. So did music. Mrs. Joyful sang a lot, and she danced as often. She would take Cat Mandoo in her arms and whirl around and around. He loved dancing. He also loved hearing the stories about famous cats that she told him. Cat Mandoo wished he could meet the Owl and the Pussy Cat, the Cat in the Hat, and Pussy Cat, Pussy Cat.

Cat Mandoo liked to hide too. And he was very good at it. Once, he hid for an entire month! That was when his humans brought him home from the animal shelter, and he was shy.

Cat Mandoo was as skilled at doing stunts as he was at hiding. He would hop like a bunny rabbit down the stairs. Then he would run up the stairs and hop down again. The happy cat liked to balance on the skinny edges of the fish tank to drink the water. He could hang upside down from chairs. And he did somersaults on top of the refrigerator.

In fact, he was entertaining himself on top of the refrigerator when he first knew that he wanted to fly. Cat Mandoo liked being up high. And he thought he would like it *even more* when he was up *even higher*.

CHAPTER 2

Cat Mandoo Tries to
Teach Himself to Fly

Near this happy home, there was a wonderful pear tree that was popular with many animals. It was Cat Mandoo's tree. And he was very good about sharing it. Birds rested there. Squirrels chased each other up and down the trunk—or from branch to branch. And raccoons climbed the tree at night to reach the pears.

When Cat Mandoo climbed his tree, squirrels would jump to another tree or onto the roof of his house. Birds would fly away.

"Come back! Come back!" he would cry out to the birds. "Teach me to fly!"

But they never returned to his pear tree while he was sitting there.

Cat Mandoo decided he would try to fly on his own. He would try to reach the roof of his house first, before aiming for the sky. Cat Mandoo climbed to the highest limb of his pear tree. He practiced moving his front paws and tail as fast as he could.

And he held his breath as long as he could—hoping to make himself lighter.

After a while, however, Cat Mandoo gave up the idea of reaching the roof. He knew his plan would not work. Not today, anyway. He would try again tomorrow.

CHAPTER 3

Cat Man and His Neighborhood Friends

Cat Mandoo heard familiar chattering coming from the ground. His neighborhood buddies were gathering in his yard. It was a big yard, but they knew just where to find him: in his pear tree, trying to figure out how to fly—or waiting for a bird to teach him.

Cat Mandoo knew his friends were going to tease him. They always did. But he was still happy to see them.

Flora the Angora announced, "You have to stop this, Cat Man." That's what his friends called him. "It isn't normal for a cat to want to fly. How many times do we have to tell you that we aren't *meant* to fly!"

Trouble the Tabby told his friend, "No bird is going to agree to teach you to fly, Cat Man. Besides, we can do so many things that other animals *can't* do. That should make you happy enough."

Said Annalise the Siamese, in her sassiest voice, "For instance, no matter how far we fall, we always land on our paws."

"And my grandmother told me we have nine lives!" whispered Cleo the Calico.

Trouble continued, "We can move so quickly that humans can't see us. We can move so quietly that they can't hear us. And Cleo's grandmother said we have nine lives!" he shouted. "Isn't *that* enough to make you happy?"

The cat called Cotton Candy—who was all white—snarled, "No, that's not enough for Cat Man. *Next,* he'll want to swim!"

Cat Mandoo's other friends quivered and shivered at the thought of being in water. But Cotton Candy didn't mind being wet. He wasn't afraid of anything. Not *this* feline! Because he had lived on the street until he was almost three. That's when his humans brought Cotton Candy into their home.

"Stop making fun of Cat Man! It's good to have dreams— even if they never come true," Cleo the clever Calico said. "The important thing is to have them." Cleo came from a very long line of very clever Calicos.

The sassy Siamese said, purring in that sassy way of hers, "Cat Man, do come down, or we will call the fire department to *get* you down!"

Cat Mandoo scurried down the trunk of his pear tree. He half-heartedly joined his pals chasing chipmunks, mice, squirrels, and birds. After some time went by, and no one—not even Cotton

Candy—had caught even *one* chipmunk, mouse, squirrel, or bird—the cats chased one another.

They tumbled to the ground and rolled around and around as cats do—until they became one enormous ball of Siamese, Tuxedo, Calico, Angora, Tabby, and white. Anyone looking on couldn't tell where one cat ended and another began.

The felines tired one another out, and they lazily lounged in the sun. When Cat Mandoo loafed and romped with them, he forgot his ambitious dream of flying.

CHAPTER 4

The Joyfuls Prepare Cat Mandoo for a Long Trip

When Cat Mandoo wasn't busy, he followed his human family around the house. On this particular day, he had nothing much to do. So he watched Mr. and Mrs. Joyful pack their suitcases. Cat Mandoo knew they were going away. What he *didn't* know was that they were taking him with them.

The very next day, Mr. Joyful told him, "We are going on a very long trip to the other side of the world. We would miss you too much if we left you at home. So you are coming with us! Won't that be fun?"

Cat Mandoo became very excited. He had never been away before. And exploring some place new was his *very* favorite kind of fun!

"Maybe we are going to London to look at the queen! Maybe Pussy Cat, Pussy Cat will be there too!" he said to himself.

Mrs. Joyful said, "We are going for a long car ride to the airport. And when we get there, we are going to go on a noisy airplane for an even *longer* ride. But I don't want you to be afraid, my sweet little boy. You know that we love you dearly—and that we would never let anything bad happen to you!"

Then she gently placed him in his carrier.

CHAPTER 5

Cat Mandoo Explores
a Strange Place

Cat Mandoo slept for a few hours. He had dreams about flying and swimming with swans, ducks, and geese. Earth looked far more interesting to Cat Mandoo from way up high. And he found that he liked the feel of water on his fur.

When Cat Man woke up from his wonderful dreams, he wanted to fly more than ever. He thought he might even learn to swim. Then Cat Mandoo realized that he was somewhere he had never been before.

"This strange place must be the airplane," he thought. His curiosity overcame him. "What is this airplane like?" Cat Mandoo wondered.

He *had* to find out! Luckily, Mr. and Mrs. Joyful were asleep. And luckily, they had not closed the door of Cat Mandoo's carrier all the way. So he did what any cat would do: He wiggled out of his carrier, and he went off to have fun.

A curtain was hanging behind his human parents and a few other passengers. It divided the front of the airplane from the main cabin. Cat Mandoo dashed under the curtain.

At first, he was afraid. The airplane was much bigger than it had seemed when he was on the other side of the curtain. And much more crowded! He had never seen so many humans before! But then, Cat Mandoo noticed that none of them were paying attention to him—and it was mostly dark—so he felt safe. The passengers were asleep or reading books, watching movies, or playing computer games.

Cat Mandoo began to explore the big airplane. He had fun scampering up and down the aisle—sniffing and looking at everything and everyone. He hadn't known that humans were all so different from one another. He noticed especially the difference in their sizes. Some people were so small that their seats looked really, really big. And others were so big that their seats looked really, really small.

"If only the seats were empty!" Cat Mandoo thought. "I would hang upside down from each and every one of them!"

CHAPTER 6

More Fun on the Airplane

Cat Mandoo was frolicking about the airplane—doing somersaults and tumbling down the *very* long aisle—when he noticed that many, many passengers were wearing sneakers. Sneakers meant shoelaces. And there were more of them than he could count! Using his teeth, he tugged at and untied all the shoelaces he could get to. He did this so quickly and quietly—as only a cat could— that no one felt or heard a thing! Cat Mandoo was very pleased with himself when he looked down the aisle at all the shoelaces he had untied.

"Good job, Cat Man!" he said to himself. And then he thought, "What fun this strange airplane is!"

While he was admiring his fine work, Cat Mandoo saw that the ends of a lot of seat belts were dangling like toys. He swatted every seat belt that wasn't buckled. He smacked and whacked them back and forth. When the seat belts would swing, Cat Mandoo would jump up and ride on them. This sport kept him busy for quite some time, and he thought, "I wish my buddies were here. They would like this place!"

CHAPTER 7

At Home in the Strange Place

A sweet scent in the air drew Cat Mandoo to a bunch of flowers on a big brim on a big hat. Under the big-brimmed hat, a big woman was snoring. He jumped up on the headrest and nibbled some of the flowers. The lady moved in her sleep, and she accidentally knocked Cat Mandoo to the floor. He landed on all four paws, naturally.

Snacking on the flowers only made him hungrier. But he forgot about that when he heard a door being opened. Cat Mandoo said to himself, "I'll just have to go and see what's on the other side of that door!"

The man who was opening the door was so large that he had to leave the room sideways. So there was more than enough time for Cat Mandoo to scoot from where he was and sneak in before the door closed.

He knew it was a bathroom right away. So he began unrolling and shredding the roll of toilet paper—just like he did at home. Somehow, the game was much more fun in *this* bathroom. Cat

Mandoo heard another passenger—a tall woman in a striped dress—opening the door. He darted out between her feet without touching her—as only cats can.

CHAPTER 8

Cat Man's Beautiful Mess

What luck! A ball of yarn was rolling toward Cat Mandoo from the far end of the airplane. He couldn't stop himself: He nudged it so it would roll away from him, and then he chased after it. When Cat Mandoo caught the ball of yarn, he pounced on it. He tumbled onto his back, and he juggled the yarn with all four paws. Then Cat Mandoo rolled the ball of yarn some more. He was having a grand time unraveling and rolling, rolling and unraveling—running up and down the *very* long aisle and pouncing and tumbling. And no one heard a thing— because, after all, he was a cat!

Cat Mandoo tickled, scratched, and rubbed himself with the yarn. He played and played until the yarn wasn't a ball any longer.

Cat Mandoo congratulated himself. What a BEAUTIFUL mess he had made! Yarn was tangled up with untied shoelaces. It was wrapped around and around many of the seat belts. It was twisted and twirled around the legs of the still-snoring woman with the big-brimmed hat—and around the legs of many other passengers. It was everywhere!

CHAPTER 9

The Runaway Cat Panics
and Is Discovered

Cat Mandoo was at the very back of the big airplane. He was terribly tired and horribly hungry. And he wanted to go someplace else—someplace where there was food. But the only doors that opened were the ones to the bathrooms. And he knew there was no way out through there. Cat Mandoo knew he was trapped. And he was not happy about this! At all! He began to meow very, very loudly. Louder than he had ever meowed before!

The passengers who were sitting at the back of the airplane were laughing or giggling or smiling. A runaway animal on an airplane was something they had never heard of!

"Do you think the runaway is a stowaway?" one of the passengers asked the others sitting in the back rows. They all laughed or giggled or smiled again.

Cat Mandoo scurried around, looking for the driver of the airplane. He planned to meow and cry and brush against his or her leg. Then maybe the driver would let him out.

But Cat Mandoo couldn't find the pilot—so he thought no one was driving the airplane. Now he was *really* unhappy—and *really* afraid. He meowed again. And again.

Cat Mandoo pretended that Cleo and Cotton Candy were there. He knew that Cotton Candy would tell him to be brave— that there was nothing to be afraid of. And Cleo would repeat what her grandmother told her about cats having nine lives. Cat Mandoo could almost hear his buddies' voices. This calmed him.

Kadwyck

CHAPTER 10

A Fun Ride on the Decorated Airplane

All of a sudden, the sun came up. It wasn't dark anymore, and the humans became restless. They noticed the yarn all around in the sunlight.

"Oh, look, the runaway cat has decorated the airplane for us!" one of them said. Her hair was blue, orange, and purple.

"And with my ball of yarn!" exclaimed a skinny elderly woman wearing a dark purple dress. "I was wondering where my yarn went!"

A tall young man wearing jeans and a baseball cap backwards tried to stand up to stretch his long legs. But he couldn't move: His shoelaces were all jumbled up with the yarn. The young man saw that the shoelaces of the man next to him were untied too. He looked across the aisle to the next row of passengers—and to the row of passengers behind them. And he saw that none of the shoelaces were tied and that purple yarn was everywhere! The young man knew exactly what had happened!

He explained to the others, "The runaway cat untied all our shoelaces and wrapped yarn around them!"

"And look at our seat belts!" merrily said a teenager with hoops through her nose and hoops through her ears. "More yarn! Wow, this cat has been busy! But are we sure there's only *one*?" She was laughing so hard that she could barely say the words. "Another cat could be hiding! Wow! I know cats. And I can tell you: When they don't want you to find them, you *can't* find them! Wow!"

"Only a cat, or cats, could have done this!" a passenger in a polka dot blouse and jeans agreed. "We are going to have to untwist the yarn from our shoelaces and untangle it from our seat belts. That's the only way we can get off the plane when it lands. But I must admit that I don't want this fun ride to end!"

A little boy wearing a bow tie and suspenders was very excited. He looked like a little grown-up—except that he was clutching a blue toy elephant. He yelled to the big woman in the big-brimmed hat, "Someone's been eating the flowers on your hat, lady! It must have been the cat!"

What a fun time the passengers were having because of Cat Mandoo!

An older man in a three-piece suit came out of the bathroom. "It looks like a pack of cats had a party in the bathroom!" he said. "But I can't guess how they got in and out of there!"

"I have never had such a good time on an airplane!" a very old man in an argyle sweater and thick-rimmed glasses said.

The other passengers agreed.

CHAPTER 11

The Chubby Child with the Grabby Hands

Cat Mandoo was more afraid than he had been since he lived at the animal shelter. It was bad enough that there was no one driving this strange airplane—and that he was terribly tired and horribly hungry. But now, the laughing and shouting were *much* too loud. These humans were *much* too noisy!

Cat Mandoo decided to run to the front of the airplane. He was going to sneak under the curtain—back to his own humans—and back into his carrier. He would be safe there! But a shrieking, chubby human child was running toward Cat Mandoo with her arms opened wide. Her chubby, grabby hands were going to pick him up. He just knew it. Cat Mandoo braced himself.

CHAPTER 12

The Feline Finally Flies

The laughing and shouting in the main cabin woke Mr. and Mrs. Joyful. Mr. Joyful reached into the carrier to pet Cat Mandoo. But he was gone! They called his name. They looked under their seats, and they looked under the seats of the passengers sitting near them. They didn't know that their fun-loving feline had caused all the excitement on the other side of the curtain.

"Where is he?" the Joyfuls asked each other.

"The only way to get out of a moving airplane is wearing a parachute," said Mr. Joyful. "And Cat Mandoo doesn't have one!"

They smiled briefly at the picture they had in their minds. It was a picture of their precious little cat—in a tiny little parachute—floating happily outside their window.

"He must be in the main cabin!" Mrs. Joyful announced, as soon as the floating feline faded from her mind.

Mr. and Mrs. Joyful pushed back the curtain, and they saw Cat Mandoo in the chubby young girl's arms.

"Are you lost, Cutie Pie?" she asked him. "My name is Celeste." She could see that he was frightened. "I used to be scared too, but I'm not anymore. It's fun to fly!"

He cuddled very close to Celeste. He put his face against her face, and he put his front paws around her neck.

"Did she say *fly*? Am I *flying*?" Cat Mandoo asked himself cheerfully.

Everyone watched as Celeste carried her newly found friend to one of the windows. "See how pretty it is!" she said with great excitement.

Cat Mandoo didn't see the ground. He saw only clouds, sunlight, and the sky.

"I really *am* flying!" he thought. "And higher than any bird ever flew! I am sure of that."

CHAPTER 13

The Airplane Adventure Ends and Perfect Dreams Begin

Mr. and Mrs. Joyful shouted Cat Mandoo's name, and they rushed over to the kind little girl.

"He is such a nice cat," Celeste said. "Can I take him home?"

"No, dear. Cat Mandoo is our little guy, and we love him dearly," Mrs. Joyful said as she held up her arms to take him. "You are so sweet. You should have a cat of your own!" she continued. "There are many, many cats in animal shelters everywhere who are longing for loving homes. I'm sure any of them would be happy to live with you."

Then she and her husband hugged Cat Mandoo really, really hard. And they gave him an especially big kiss.

Everyone on the airplane clapped.

The Joyfuls walked back to their seats on the other side of the curtain. This time, they were *extremely* careful when they tucked their tuckered-out Tuxedo back into his carrier.

Cat Mandoo was very tired after his big adventure. He fell asleep right away. Almost. Before he did, he said to himself, "Wait till my buddies back home hear that I can fly! I'll be the most popular cat in the neighborhood!"

Then he had the sweetest, most perfect dreams ever. After all, he was the cat's meow!

The author would like you to know that the "cat's meow" means the very best. Sometimes people say the "cat's pajamas" or the "cat's whiskers" instead.

ABOUT THE AUTHOR

Alexis Kasden has been writing since she was ten. Her favorite form of fiction is the short story for children, because she feels that the most charming and artfully crafted pieces can lead children to become readers and dreamers and can encourage them to be socially responsible.

For twenty years, she worked for Grolier Incorporated, the oldest publishing company in the United States, first as art editor on *The New Book of Knowledge*, the acclaimed encyclopedia for children, and then as head of corporate communications. Her duties included designing and developing programs for children in the community and serving as editor in chief for the in-house publication for employees, which carried news from corporate headquarters and the company's subsidiaries, imprints, and worldwide branches.

Ms. Kasden has been a devoted animal rights advocate since 1960, at which time, she remembers, most people didn't believe that animals had feelings at all and, consequently, did not deserve to have rights. She has written, and continues to write, letters of thanks, protest, or suggestions to prime ministers and presidents of countries; CEOs of companies, both here and abroad; and US government officials. The author is heartened by her observation that the general population, in great measure, continues to develop a heightened sense of obligation to improve the lives of animals. She hopes that you have a pet you love as much as the Joyfuls love Cat Mandoo.

One of fourteen children and an aunt to twenty-three nieces and nephews, Ms. Kasden earned her master's degree in the education of the gifted from Suffolk University (Boston). She and her husband of thirty-eight years, Allen, a retired construction executive, have lived in numerous states and countries.

CPSIA information can be obtained
at www.ICGtesting.com
Printed in the USA
BVHW020016311219
568190BV00001BA/1/P

9 781684 563401